SKYLANDERS® SUPERCHARGERS

Secret Agent Secrets Part 2

Written by: **Ron Marz & David A. Rodriguez**
Art by: **Fico Ossio**
Cover Art by: **Fico Ossio**
Colors by: **David Garcia Cruz**
Letters by: **Deron Bennett**

ABDO Spotlight IDW

ABDOPUBLISHING.COM

Reinforced library bound edition published in 2018 by Spotlight, a division of ABDO PO Box 398166, Minneapolis, Minnesota 55439. Spotlight produces high-quality reinforced library bound editions for schools and libraries.
Published by agreement with IDW.

Printed in the United States of America, North Mankato, Minnesota.
042017
092017

THIS BOOK CONTAINS RECYCLED MATERIALS

Originally published as SKYLANDERS SUPERCHARGERS issue #2: Secret Agent Secrets Part 2.

PUBLISHER'S CATALOGING IN PUBLICATION DATA

Names: Marz, Ron ; Rodriguez, David A., authors. | Ossio, Fico ; Lawrence, Jack ; Cruz, David Garcia ; Zarate, Ander, illustrators.
Title: Secret Agent Secrets / writers: Ron Marz ; David A. Rodriguez ; art: Fico Ossio ; Jack Lawrence ; David Garcia Cruz ; Ander Zarate.
Description: Reinforced library bound edition. | Minneapolis, Minnesota : Spotlight, 2018. | Series: Skylanders: superchargers
Summary: Superchargers Stormblade, Nightfall, and Spitfire team up to discover why Skylanders Elite squad of Boomer, Voodood, and Ghost Roaster went missing, but the new team uncovers more than they bargained for when they're captured by Lord Spellslamzer and have to settle their differences if they hope to survive. Readers will also learn the origins of Spitfire, Smash Hit, and Fiesta.
Identifiers: LCCN 2017931204 | ISBN 9781532140396 (part 1, lib. bdg.) | ISBN 9781532140402 (part 2, lib. bdg.) | ISBN 9781532140419 (part 3, lib. bdg.)
Subjects: LCSH: Skylanders (Fictitious characters)--Juvenile fiction. | Comic books, strips, etc.--Juvenile fiction. | Graphic novels--Juvenile fiction.
Classification: DDC 741.5--dc23
LC record available at https://lccn.loc.gov/2017931204

Spotlight

A Division of ABDO
abdopublishing.com

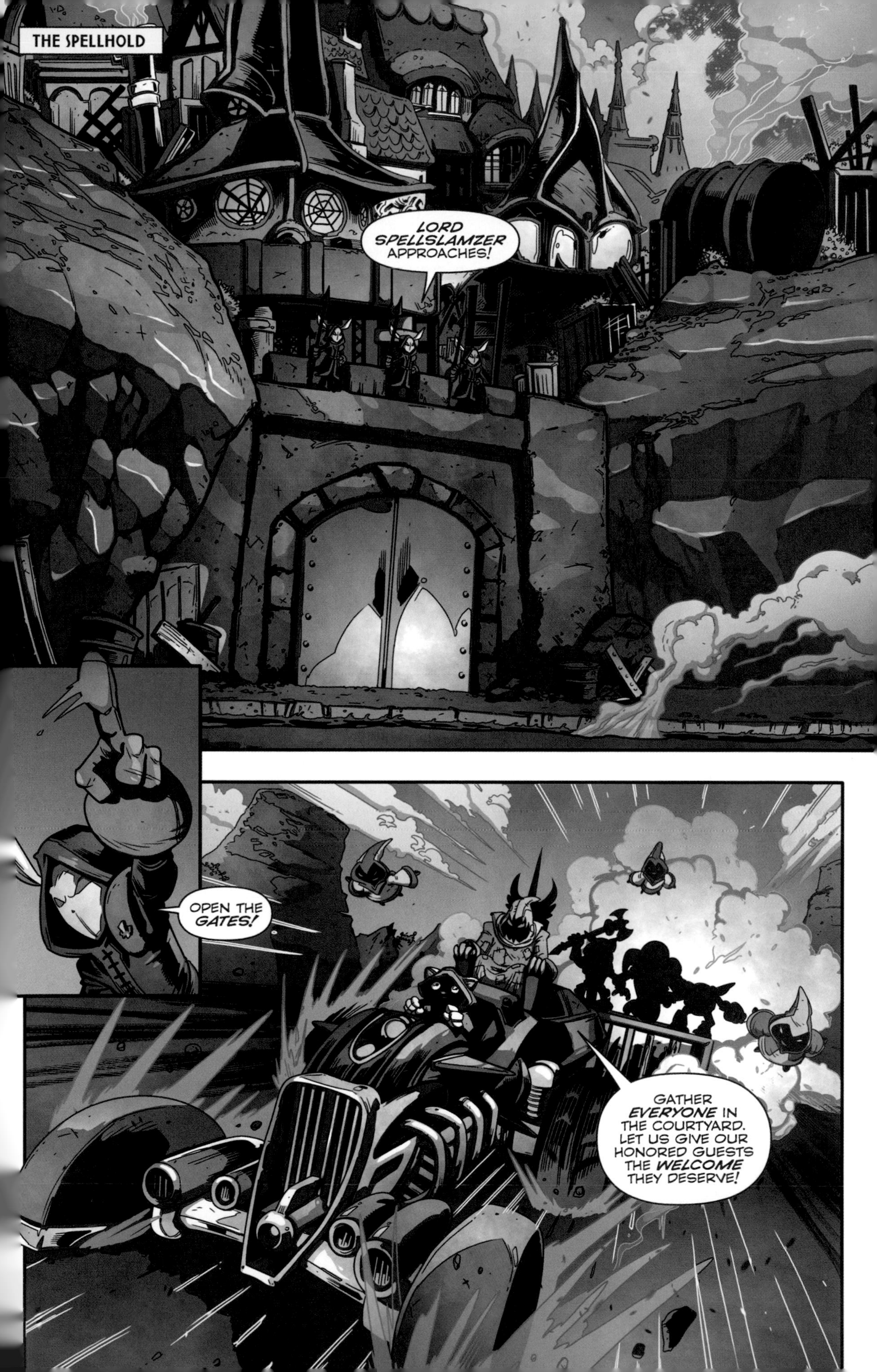
THE SPELLHOLD
LORD SPELLSLAMZER APPROACHES!
OPEN THE GATES!
GATHER EVERYONE IN THE COURTYARD. LET US GIVE OUR HONORED GUESTS THE WELCOME THEY DESERVE!

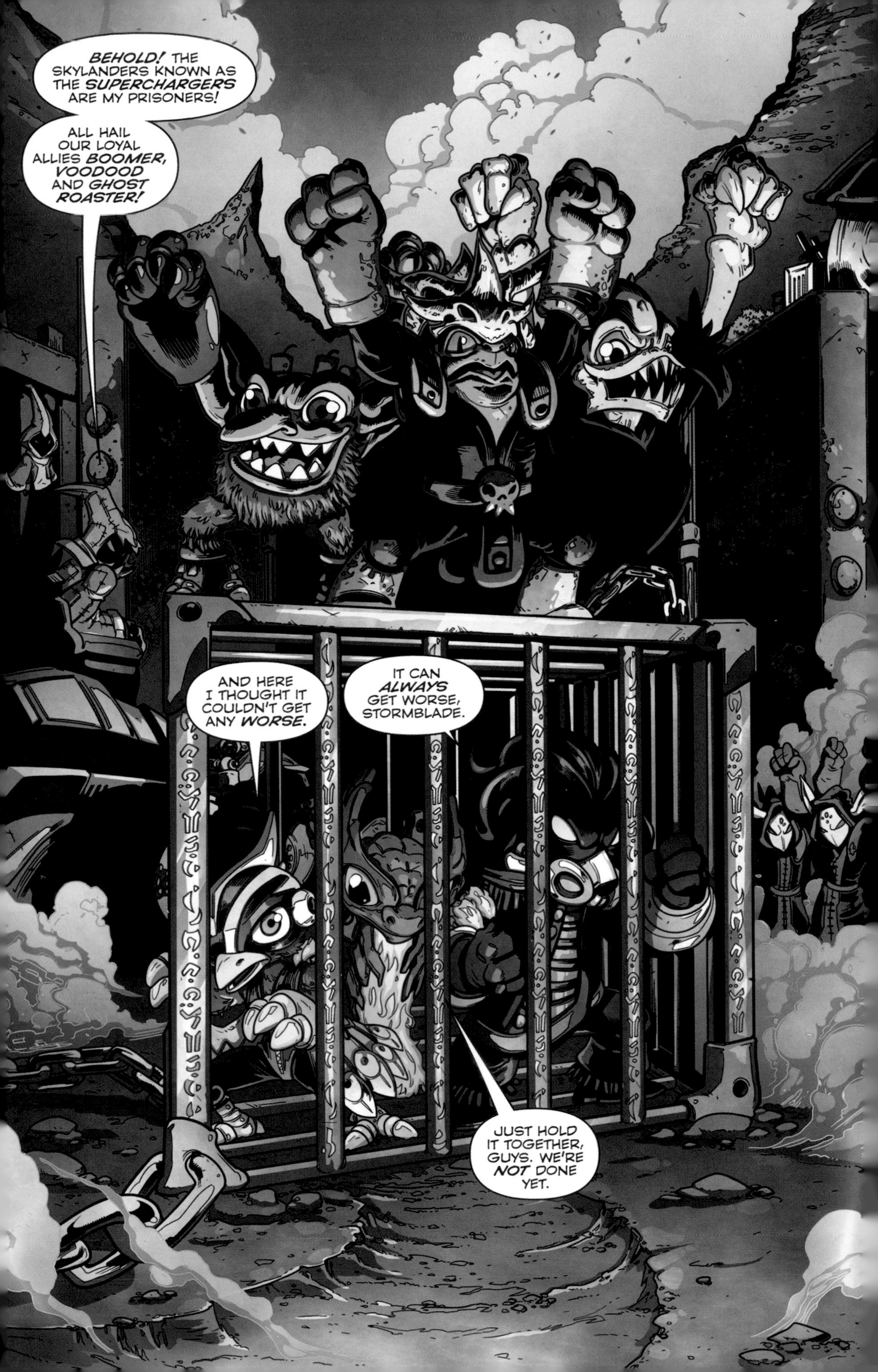
BEHOLD! THE SKYLANDERS KNOWN AS THE SUPERCHARGERS ARE MY PRISONERS!
ALL HAIL OUR LOYAL ALLIES BOOMER, VOODOOD AND GHOST ROASTER!
AND HERE I THOUGHT IT COULDN'T GET ANY WORSE.
IT CAN ALWAYS GET WORSE, STORMBLADE.
JUST HOLD IT TOGETHER, GUYS. WE'RE NOT DONE YET.

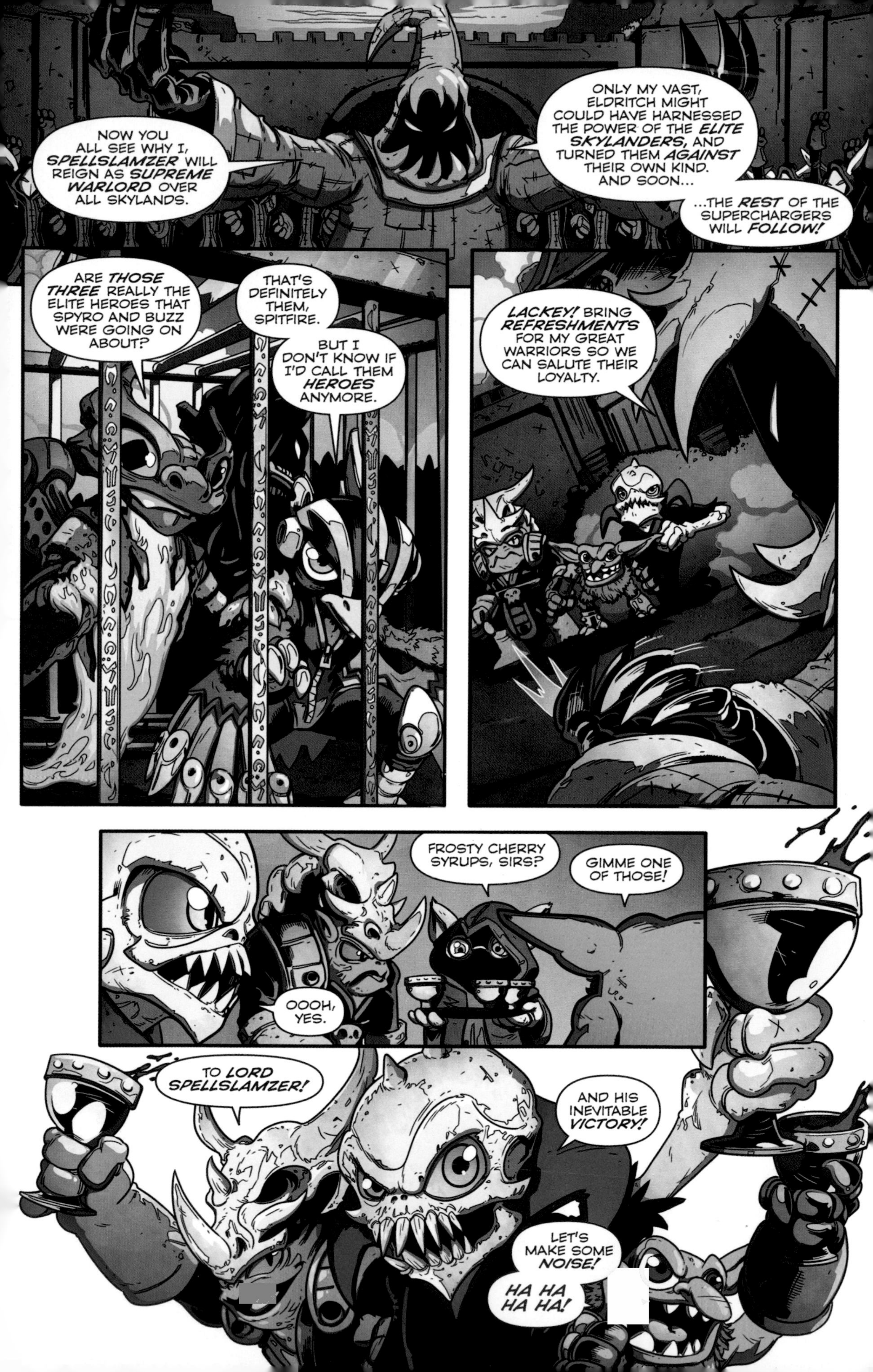
NOW YOU ALL SEE WHY I, SPELLSLAMZER WILL REIGN AS SUPREME WARLORD OVER ALL SKYLANDS.
ONLY MY VAST, ELDRITCH MIGHT COULD HAVE HARNESSED THE POWER OF THE ELITE SKYLANDERS, AND TURNED THEM AGAINST THEIR OWN KIND. AND SOON...
...THE REST OF THE SUPERCHARGERS WILL FOLLOW!
ARE THOSE THREE REALLY THE ELITE HEROES THAT SPYRO AND BUZZ WERE GOING ON ABOUT?
THAT'S DEFINITELY THEM, SPITFIRE.
BUT I DON'T KNOW IF I'D CALL THEM HEROES ANYMORE.
LACKEY! BRING REFRESHMENTS FOR MY GREAT WARRIORS SO WE CAN SALUTE THEIR LOYALTY.
FROSTY CHERRY SYRUPS, SIRS?
GIMME ONE OF THOSE!
OOOH, YES.
TO LORD SPELLSLAMZER!
AND HIS INEVITABLE VICTORY!
LET'S MAKE SOME NOISE!
HA HA HA HA!

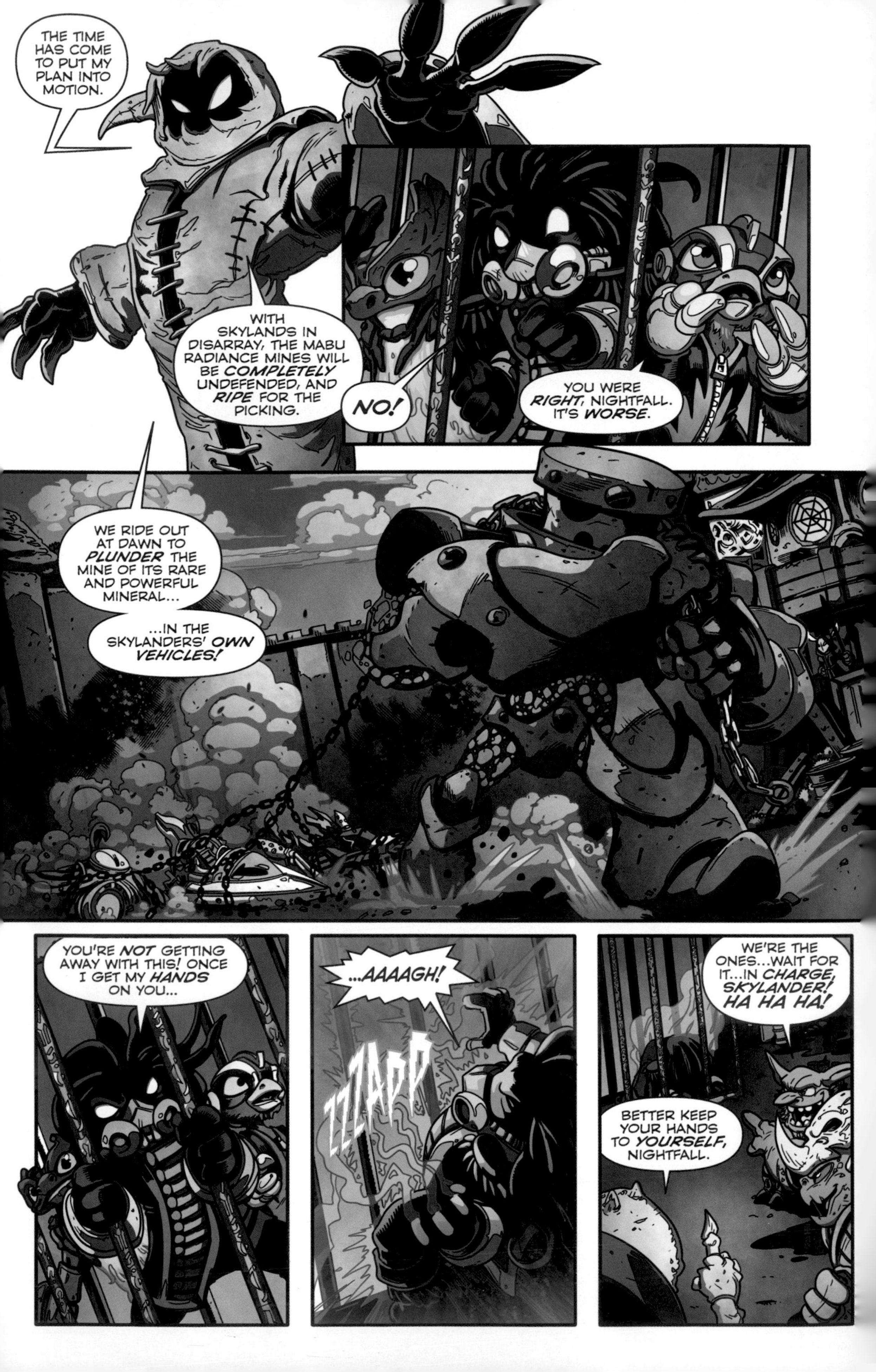
THE TIME HAS COME TO PUT MY PLAN INTO MOTION.
WITH SKYLANDS IN DISARRAY, THE MABU RADIANCE MINES WILL BE COMPLETELY UNDEFENDED, AND RIPE FOR THE PICKING.
NO!
YOU WERE RIGHT, NIGHTFALL. IT'S WORSE.
WE RIDE OUT AT DAWN TO PLUNDER THE MINE OF ITS RARE AND POWERFUL MINERAL...
...IN THE SKYLANDERS' OWN VEHICLES!
YOU'RE NOT GETTING AWAY WITH THIS! ONCE I GET MY HANDS ON YOU...
...AAAAGH!
ZZZAPP
WE'RE THE ONES...WAIT FOR IT...IN CHARGE, SKYLANDER! HA HA HA!
BETTER KEEP YOUR HANDS TO YOURSELF, NIGHTFALL.

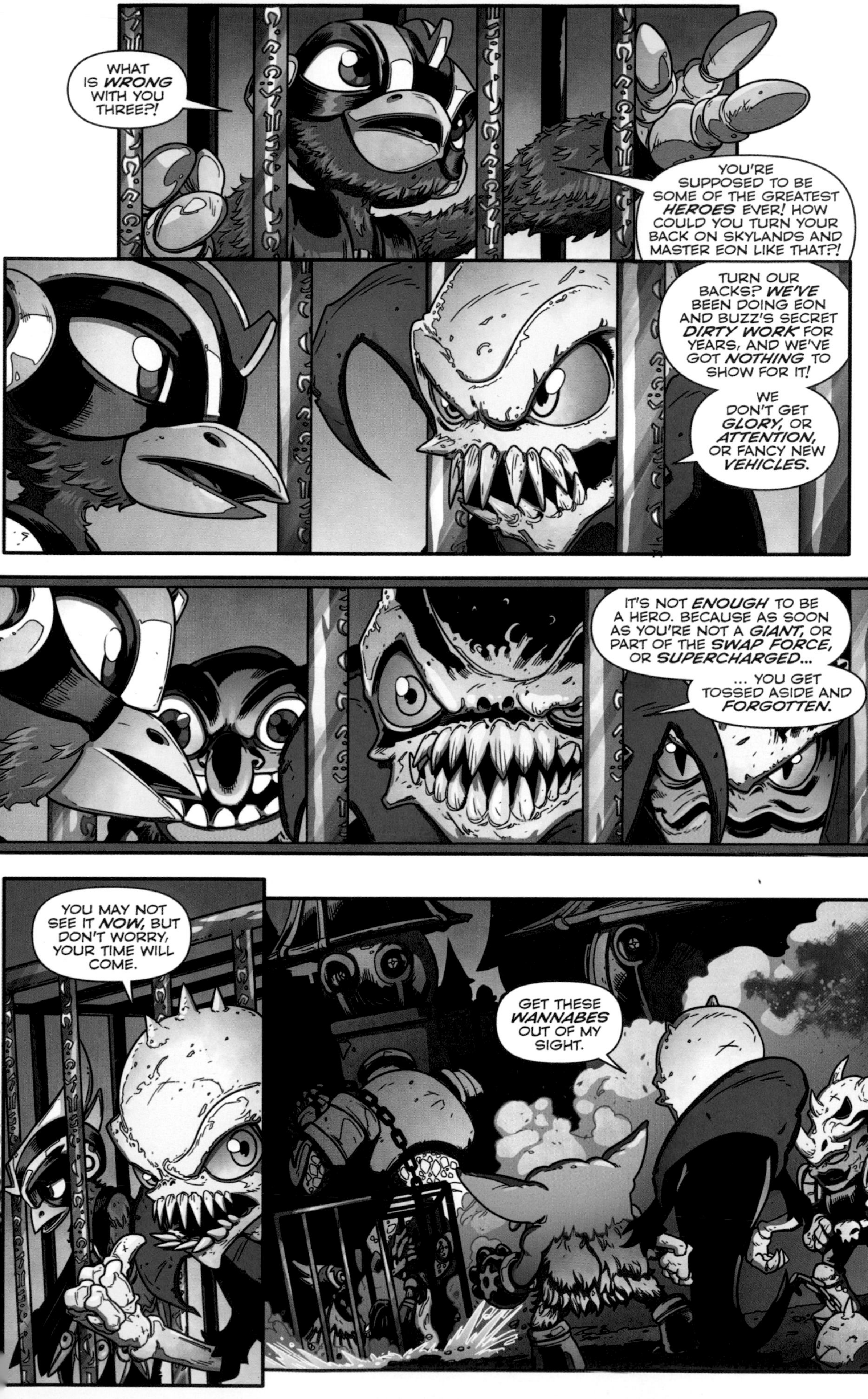
WHAT IS *WRONG* WITH YOU THREE?!
YOU'RE SUPPOSED TO BE SOME OF THE GREATEST *HEROES* EVER! HOW COULD YOU TURN YOUR BACK ON SKYLANDS AND MASTER EON LIKE THAT?!
TURN OUR BACKS? *WE'VE* BEEN DOING EON AND BUZZ'S SECRET *DIRTY WORK* FOR YEARS, AND WE'VE GOT *NOTHING* TO SHOW FOR IT!
WE DON'T GET *GLORY,* OR *ATTENTION,* OR FANCY NEW *VEHICLES.*
IT'S NOT *ENOUGH* TO BE A HERO. BECAUSE AS SOON AS YOU'RE NOT A *GIANT,* OR PART OF THE *SWAP FORCE,* OR *SUPERCHARGED...*
... YOU GET TOSSED ASIDE AND *FORGOTTEN.*
YOU MAY NOT SEE IT *NOW,* BUT DON'T WORRY, YOUR TIME WILL COME.
GET THESE *WANNABES* OUT OF MY SIGHT.

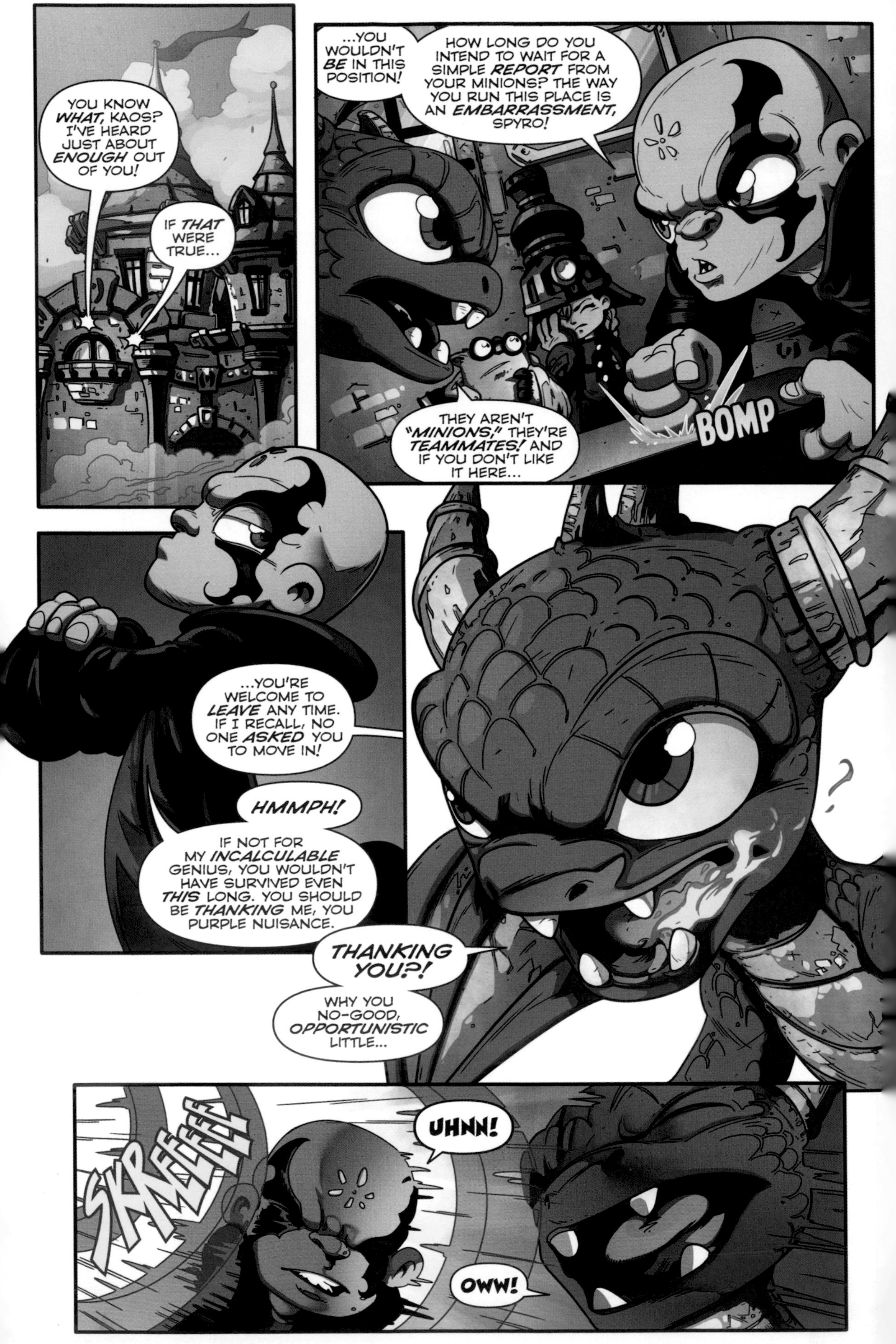
YOU KNOW WHAT, KAOS? I'VE HEARD JUST ABOUT ENOUGH OUT OF YOU!
IF THAT WERE TRUE...
...YOU WOULDN'T BE IN THIS POSITION!
HOW LONG DO YOU INTEND TO WAIT FOR A SIMPLE REPORT FROM YOUR MINIONS? THE WAY YOU RUN THIS PLACE IS AN EMBARRASSMENT, SPYRO!
BOMP
THEY AREN'T "MINIONS," THEY'RE TEAMMATES! AND IF YOU DON'T LIKE IT HERE...
...YOU'RE WELCOME TO LEAVE ANY TIME. IF I RECALL, NO ONE ASKED YOU TO MOVE IN!
HMMPH!
IF NOT FOR MY INCALCULABLE GENIUS, YOU WOULDN'T HAVE SURVIVED EVEN THIS LONG. YOU SHOULD BE THANKING ME, YOU PURPLE NUISANCE.
THANKING YOU?!
WHY YOU NO-GOOD, OPPORTUNISTIC LITTLE...
SKREEEEE
UHNN!
OWW!

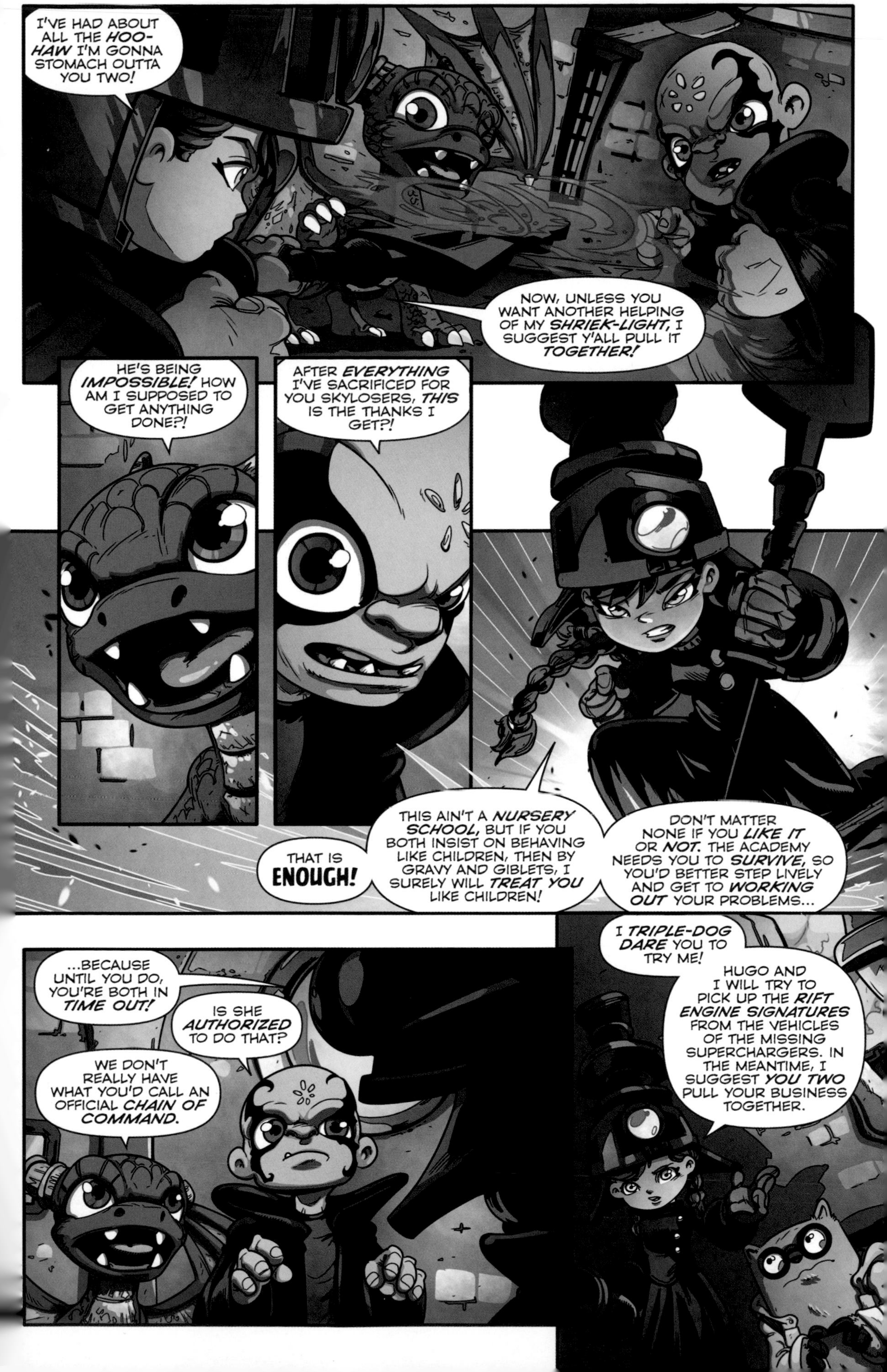
I'VE HAD ABOUT ALL THE HOO-HAW I'M GONNA STOMACH OUTTA YOU TWO!
NOW, UNLESS YOU WANT ANOTHER HELPING OF MY SHRIEK-LIGHT, I SUGGEST Y'ALL PULL IT TOGETHER!
HE'S BEING IMPOSSIBLE! HOW AM I SUPPOSED TO GET ANYTHING DONE?!
AFTER EVERYTHING I'VE SACRIFICED FOR YOU SKYLOSERS, THIS IS THE THANKS I GET?!
THAT IS ENOUGH!
THIS AIN'T A NURSERY SCHOOL, BUT IF YOU BOTH INSIST ON BEHAVING LIKE CHILDREN, THEN BY GRAVY AND GIBLETS, I SURELY WILL TREAT YOU LIKE CHILDREN!
DON'T MATTER NONE IF YOU LIKE IT OR NOT. THE ACADEMY NEEDS YOU TO SURVIVE, SO YOU'D BETTER STEP LIVELY AND GET TO WORKING OUT YOUR PROBLEMS...
...BECAUSE UNTIL YOU DO, YOU'RE BOTH IN TIME OUT!
IS SHE AUTHORIZED TO DO THAT?
WE DON'T REALLY HAVE WHAT YOU'D CALL AN OFFICIAL CHAIN OF COMMAND.
I TRIPLE-DOG DARE YOU TO TRY ME!
HUGO AND I WILL TRY TO PICK UP THE RIFT ENGINE SIGNATURES FROM THE VEHICLES OF THE MISSING SUPERCHARGERS. IN THE MEANTIME, I SUGGEST YOU TWO PULL YOUR BUSINESS TOGETHER.

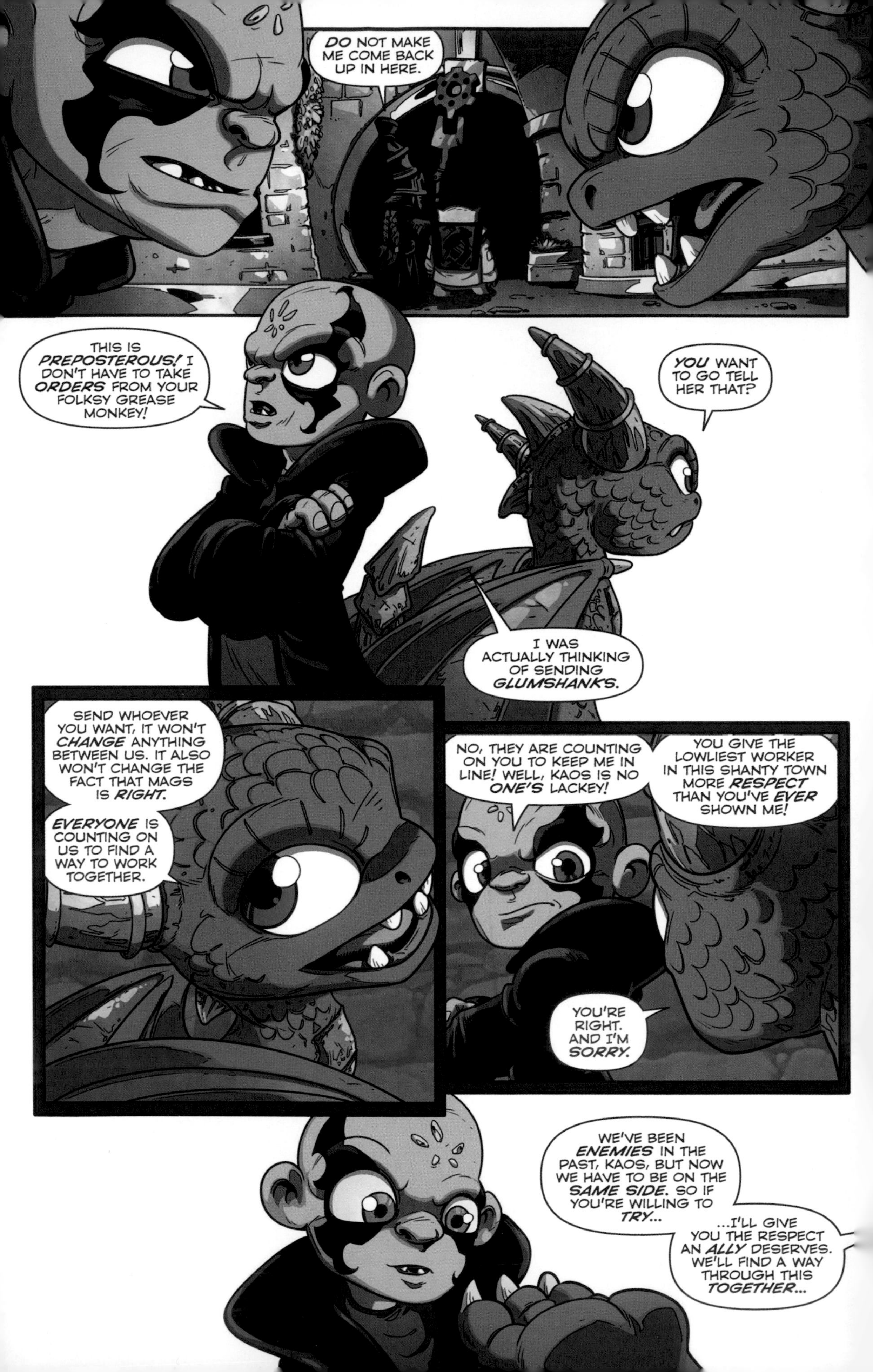
DO NOT MAKE ME COME BACK UP IN HERE.
THIS IS PREPOSTEROUS! I DON'T HAVE TO TAKE ORDERS FROM YOUR FOLKSY GREASE MONKEY!
YOU WANT TO GO TELL HER THAT?
I WAS ACTUALLY THINKING OF SENDING GLUMSHANKS.
SEND WHOEVER YOU WANT, IT WON'T CHANGE ANYTHING BETWEEN US. IT ALSO WON'T CHANGE THE FACT THAT MAGS IS RIGHT.
EVERYONE IS COUNTING ON US TO FIND A WAY TO WORK TOGETHER.
NO, THEY ARE COUNTING ON YOU TO KEEP ME IN LINE! WELL, KAOS IS NO ONE'S LACKEY!
YOU GIVE THE LOWLIEST WORKER IN THIS SHANTY TOWN MORE RESPECT THAN YOU'VE EVER SHOWN ME!
YOU'RE RIGHT. AND I'M SORRY.
WE'VE BEEN ENEMIES IN THE PAST, KAOS, BUT NOW WE HAVE TO BE ON THE SAME SIDE. SO IF YOU'RE WILLING TO TRY...
...I'LL GIVE YOU THE RESPECT AN ALLY DESERVES. WE'LL FIND A WAY THROUGH THIS TOGETHER...

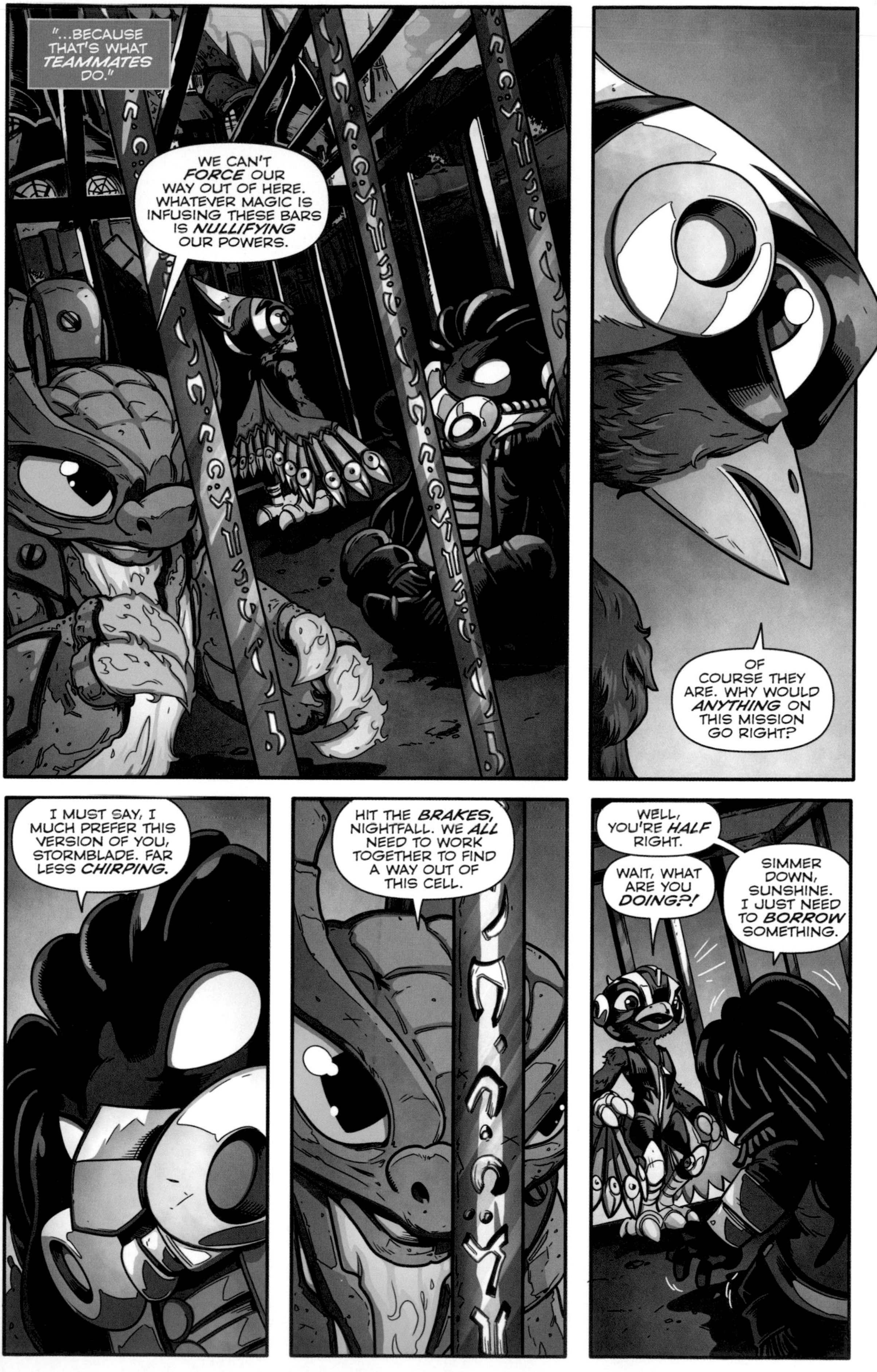
"...BECAUSE THAT'S WHAT *TEAMMATES* DO."
WE CAN'T *FORCE* OUR WAY OUT OF HERE. WHATEVER MAGIC IS INFUSING THESE BARS IS *NULLIFYING* OUR POWERS.
OF COURSE THEY ARE. WHY WOULD *ANYTHING* ON THIS MISSION GO RIGHT?
I MUST SAY, I MUCH PREFER THIS VERSION OF YOU, STORMBLADE. FAR LESS *CHIRPING*.
HIT THE *BRAKES*, NIGHTFALL. WE *ALL* NEED TO WORK TOGETHER TO FIND A WAY OUT OF THIS CELL.
WELL, YOU'RE *HALF* RIGHT.
WAIT, WHAT ARE YOU *DOING?!*
SIMMER DOWN, SUNSHINE. I JUST NEED TO *BORROW* SOMETHING.

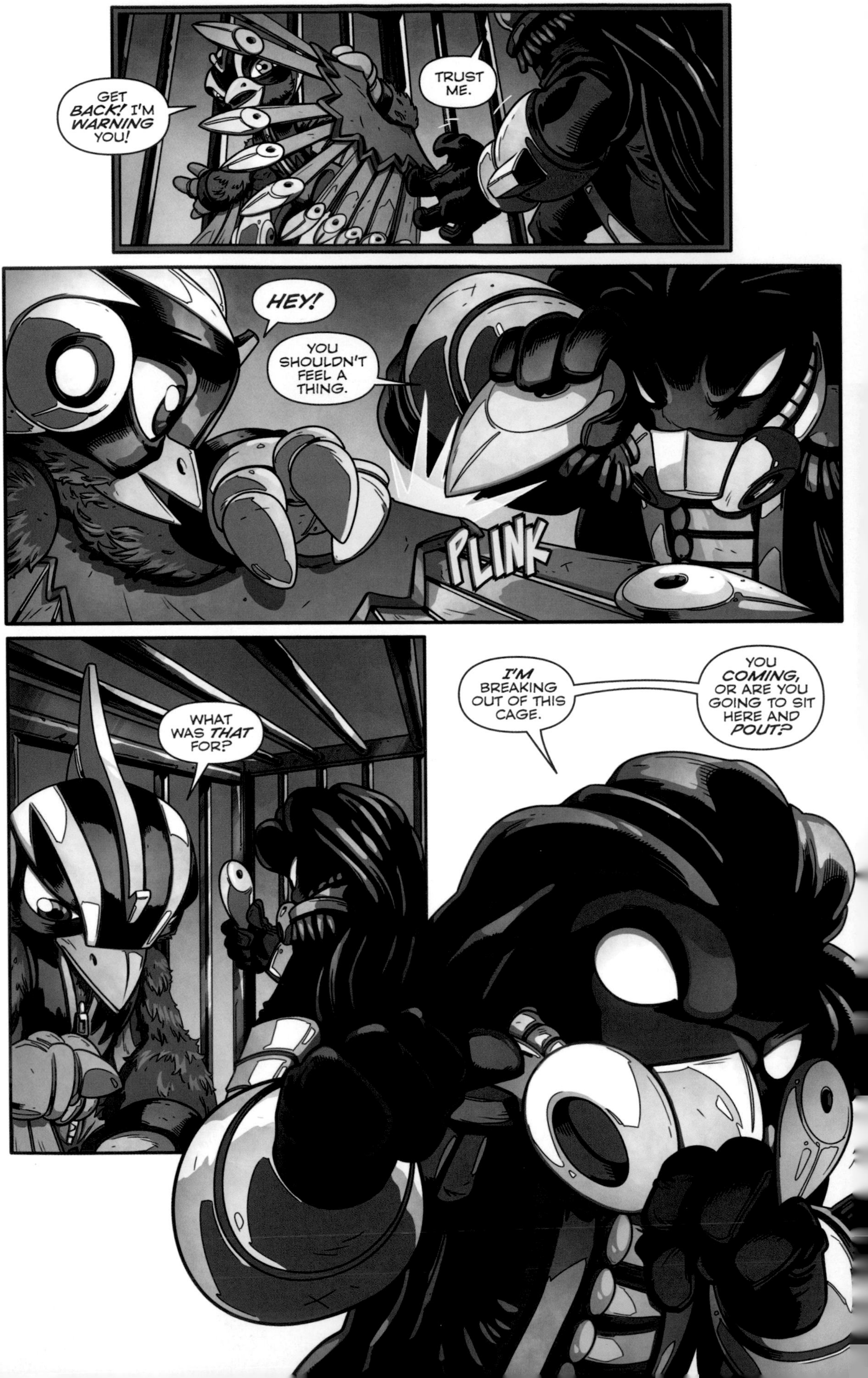
GET BACK! I'M WARNING YOU!
TRUST ME.
HEY!
YOU SHOULDN'T FEEL A THING.
PLINK
WHAT WAS THAT FOR?
I'M BREAKING OUT OF THIS CAGE.
YOU COMING, OR ARE YOU GOING TO SIT HERE AND POUT?

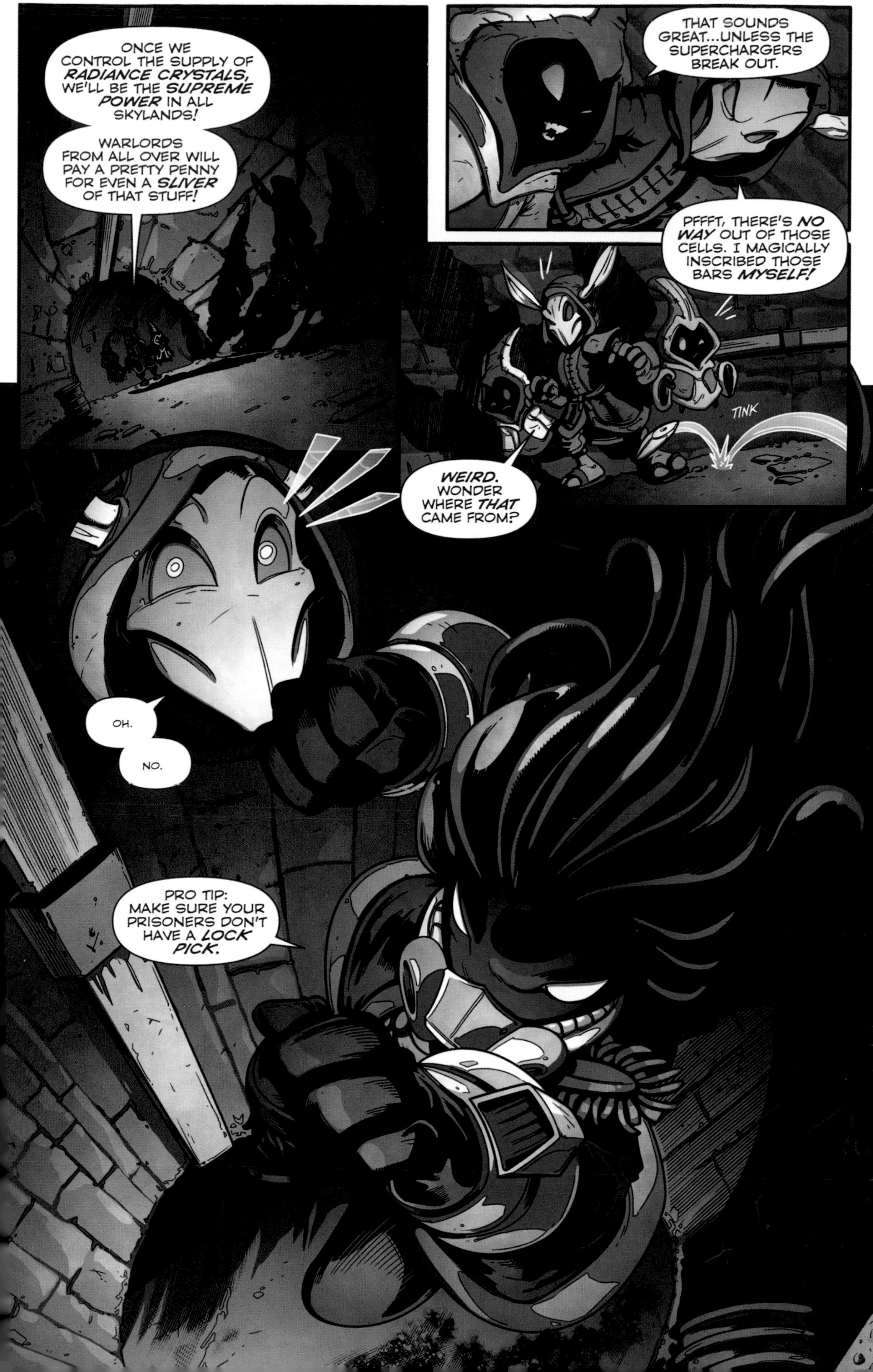

ONCE WE CONTROL THE SUPPLY OF *RADIANCE CRYSTALS,* WE'LL BE THE *SUPREME POWER* IN ALL SKYLANDS!
WARLORDS FROM ALL OVER WILL PAY A PRETTY PENNY FOR EVEN A *SLIVER* OF THAT STUFF!
THAT SOUNDS GREAT...UNLESS THE SUPERCHARGERS BREAK OUT.
PFFFT, THERE'S *NO WAY* OUT OF THOSE CELLS. I MAGICALLY INSCRIBED THOSE BARS *MYSELF!*
TINK
WEIRD. WONDER WHERE *THAT* CAME FROM?
OH.
NO.
PRO TIP: MAKE SURE YOUR PRISONERS DON'T HAVE A *LOCK PICK.*

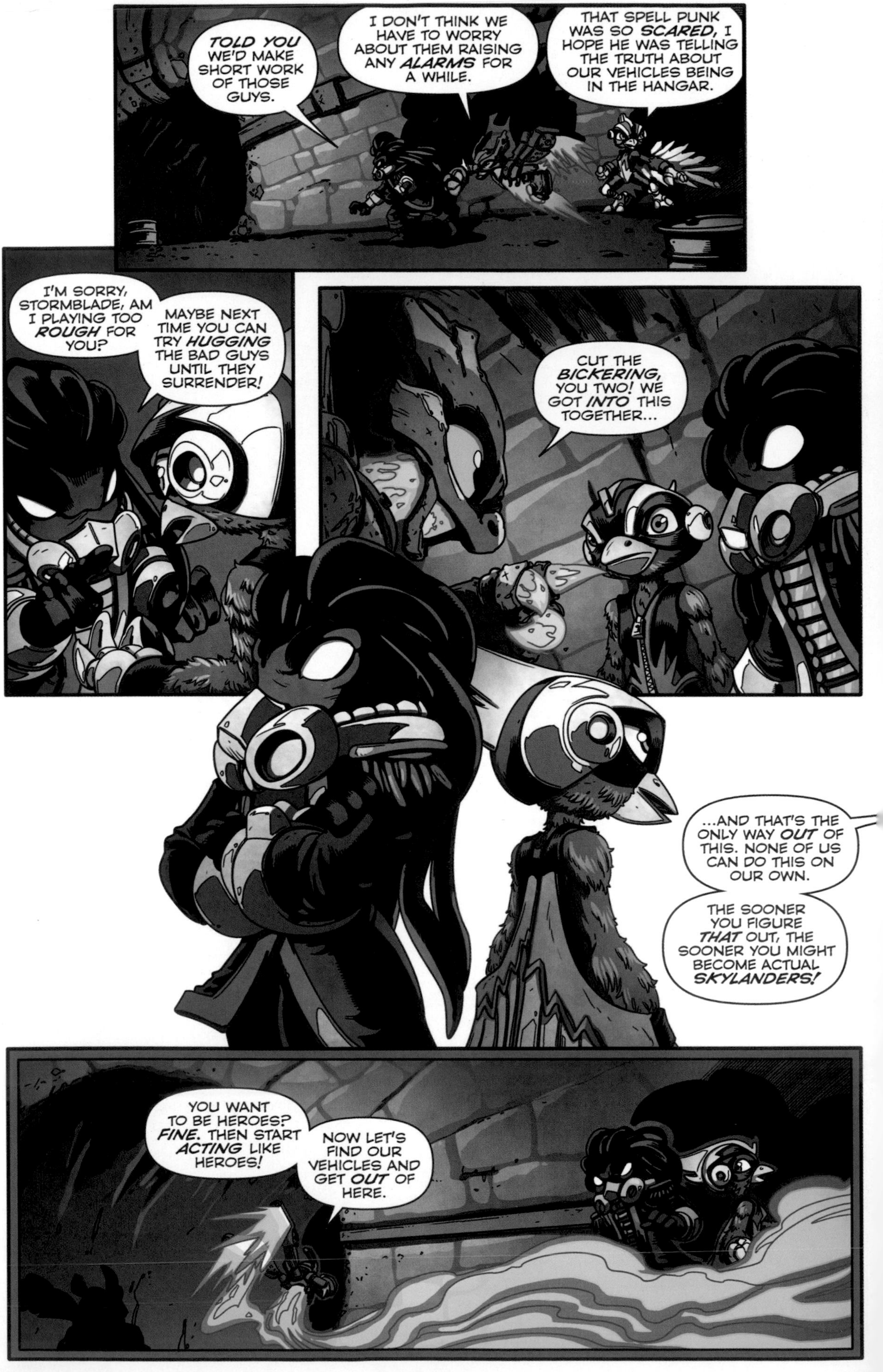
TOLD YOU WE'D MAKE SHORT WORK OF THOSE GUYS.
I DON'T THINK WE HAVE TO WORRY ABOUT THEM RAISING ANY ALARMS FOR A WHILE.
THAT SPELL PUNK WAS SO SCARED, I HOPE HE WAS TELLING THE TRUTH ABOUT OUR VEHICLES BEING IN THE HANGAR.
I'M SORRY, STORMBLADE, AM I PLAYING TOO ROUGH FOR YOU?
MAYBE NEXT TIME YOU CAN TRY HUGGING THE BAD GUYS UNTIL THEY SURRENDER!
CUT THE BICKERING, YOU TWO! WE GOT INTO THIS TOGETHER...
...AND THAT'S THE ONLY WAY OUT OF THIS. NONE OF US CAN DO THIS ON OUR OWN.
THE SOONER YOU FIGURE THAT OUT, THE SOONER YOU MIGHT BECOME ACTUAL SKYLANDERS!
YOU WANT TO BE HEROES? FINE. THEN START ACTING LIKE HEROES!
NOW LET'S FIND OUR VEHICLES AND GET OUT OF HERE.

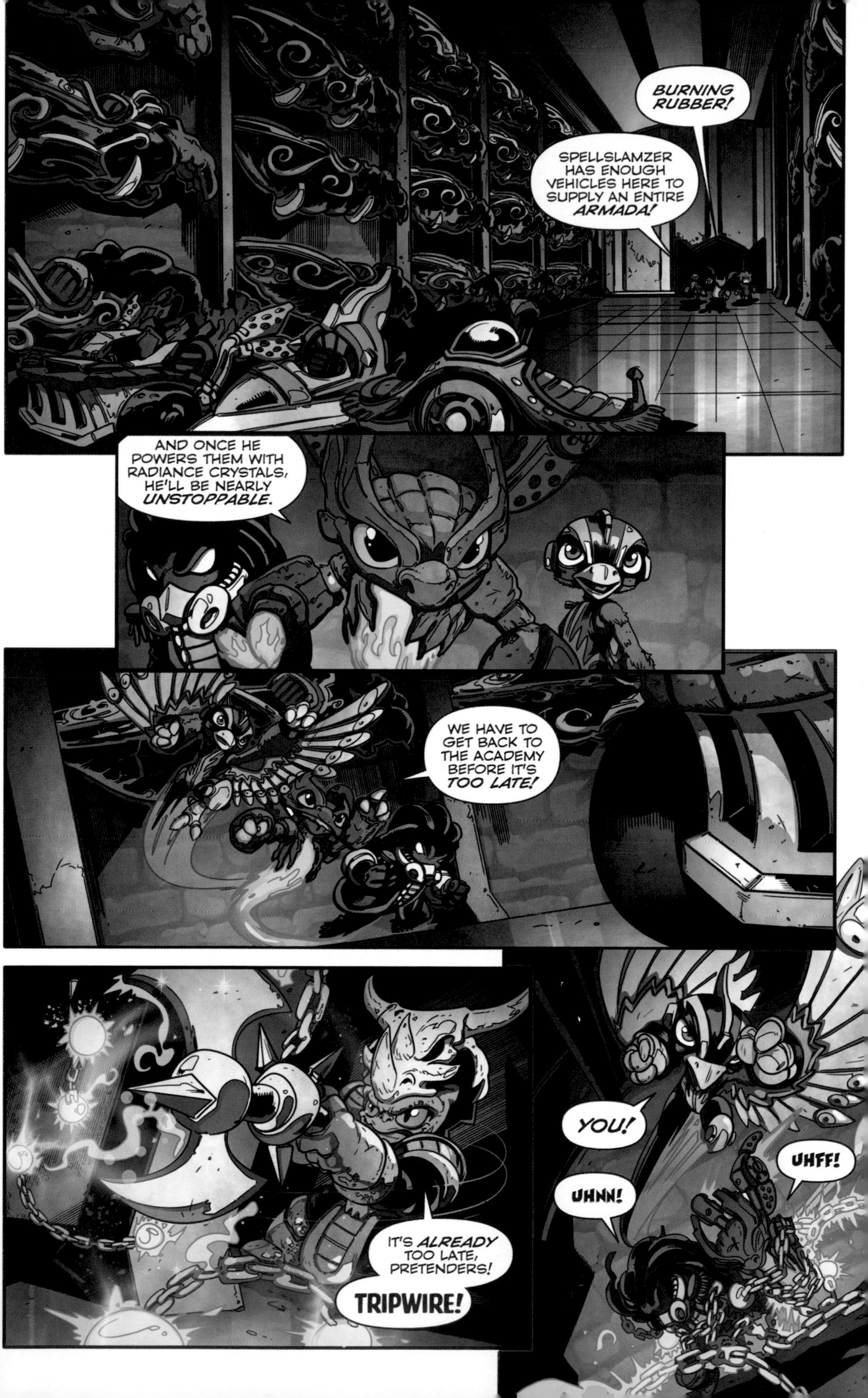
BURNING RUBBER!
SPELLSLAMZER HAS ENOUGH VEHICLES HERE TO SUPPLY AN ENTIRE ARMADA!
AND ONCE HE POWERS THEM WITH RADIANCE CRYSTALS, HE'LL BE NEARLY UNSTOPPABLE.
WE HAVE TO GET BACK TO THE ACADEMY BEFORE IT'S TOO LATE!
IT'S ALREADY TOO LATE, PRETENDERS!
TRIPWIRE!
YOU!
UHFF!
UHNN!

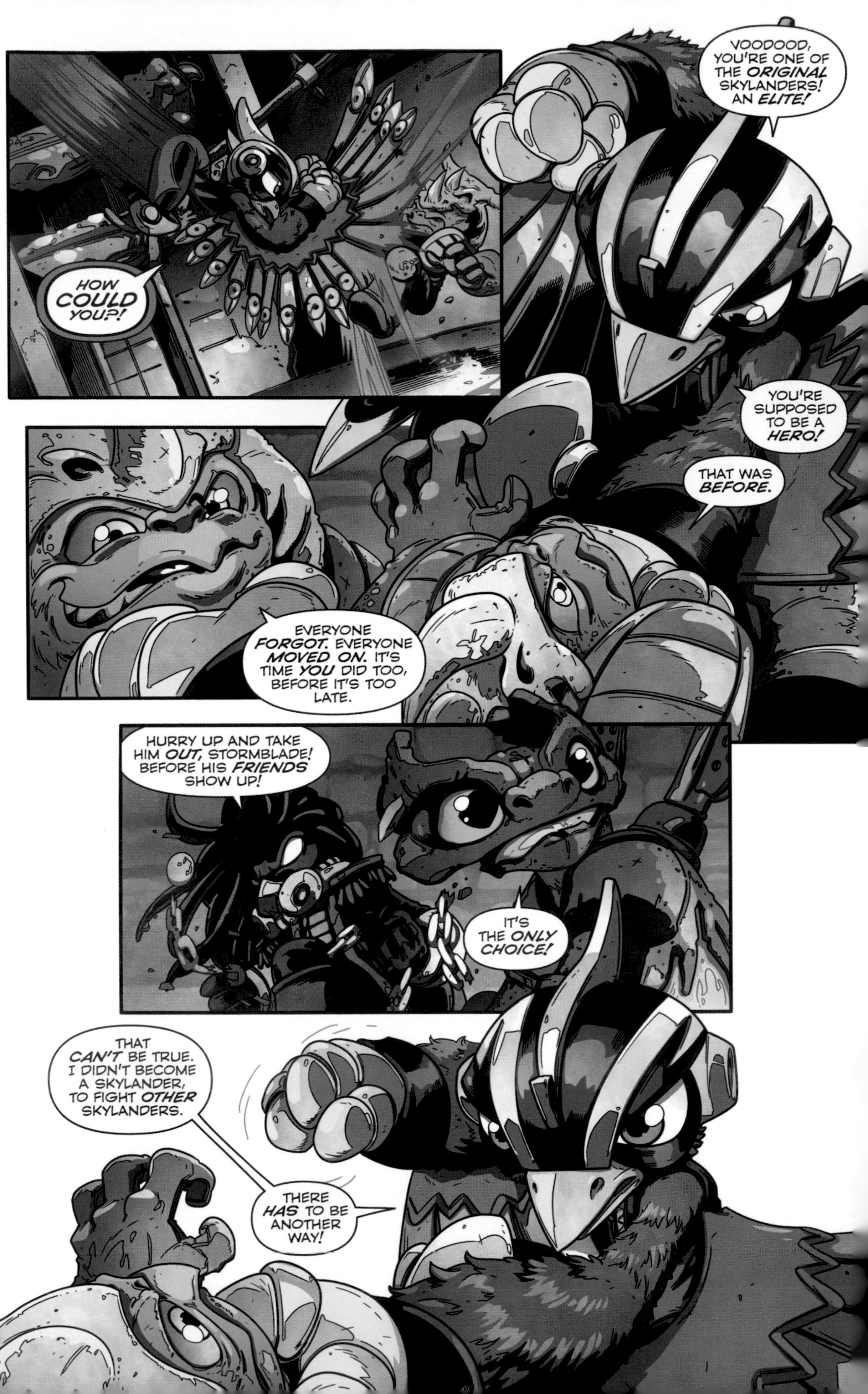
HOW COULD YOU?!
VOODOOD, YOU'RE ONE OF THE ORIGINAL SKYLANDERS! AN ELITE!
YOU'RE SUPPOSED TO BE A HERO!
THAT WAS BEFORE.
EVERYONE FORGOT. EVERYONE MOVED ON. IT'S TIME YOU DID TOO, BEFORE IT'S TOO LATE.
HURRY UP AND TAKE HIM OUT, STORMBLADE! BEFORE HIS FRIENDS SHOW UP!
IT'S THE ONLY CHOICE!
THAT CAN'T BE TRUE. I DIDN'T BECOME A SKYLANDER, TO FIGHT OTHER SKYLANDERS.
THERE HAS TO BE ANOTHER WAY!

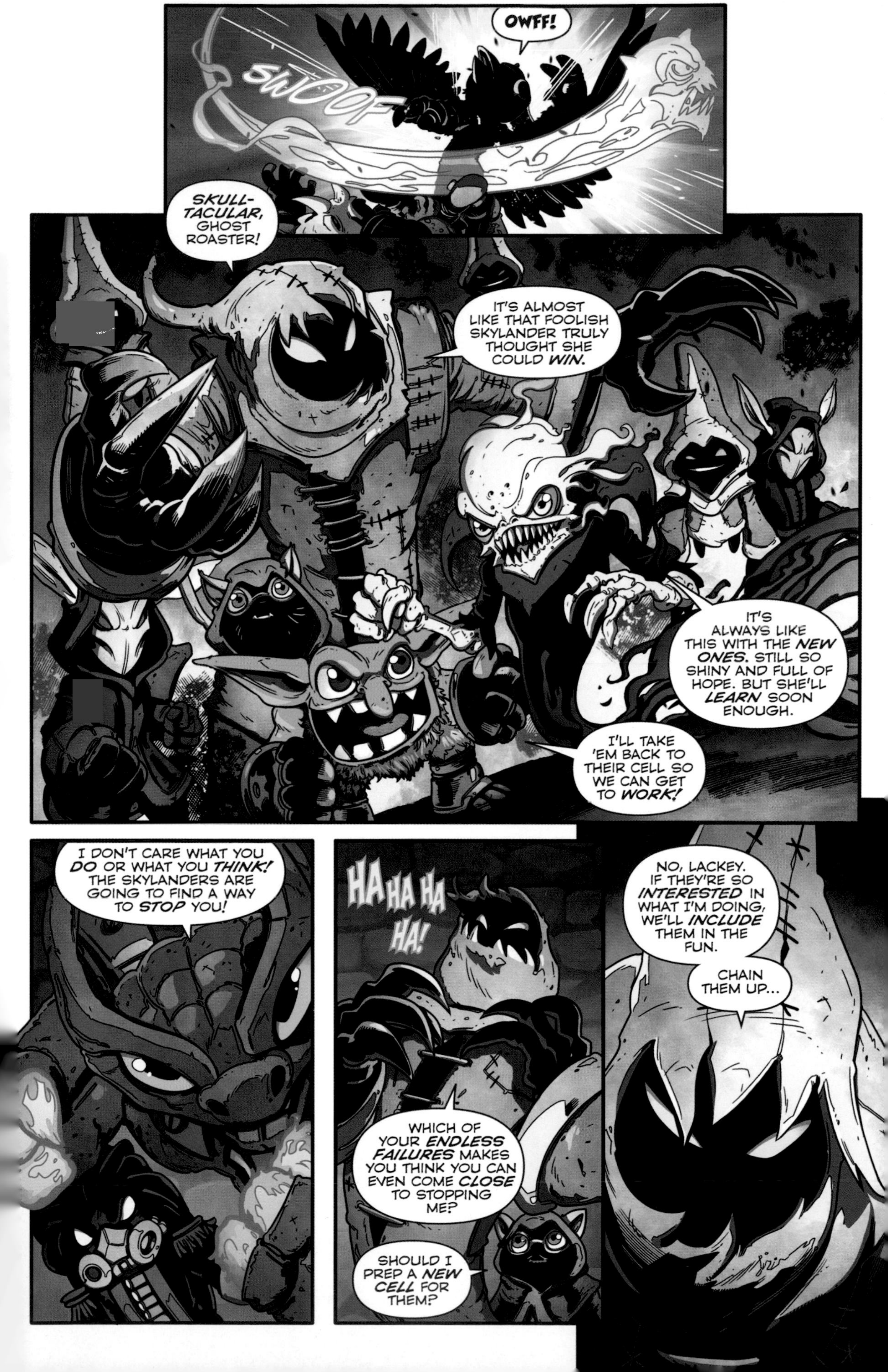
OWFF!
SWOOF
SKULL-TACULAR, GHOST ROASTER!
IT'S ALMOST LIKE THAT FOOLISH SKYLANDER TRULY THOUGHT SHE COULD WIN.
IT'S ALWAYS LIKE THIS WITH THE NEW ONES. STILL SO SHINY AND FULL OF HOPE. BUT SHE'LL LEARN SOON ENOUGH.
I'LL TAKE 'EM BACK TO THEIR CELL SO WE CAN GET TO WORK!
I DON'T CARE WHAT YOU DO OR WHAT YOU THINK! THE SKYLANDERS ARE GOING TO FIND A WAY TO STOP YOU!
HA HA HA HA HA!
WHICH OF YOUR ENDLESS FAILURES MAKES YOU THINK YOU CAN EVEN COME CLOSE TO STOPPING ME?
SHOULD I PREP A NEW CELL FOR THEM?
NO, LACKEY. IF THEY'RE SO INTERESTED IN WHAT I'M DOING, WE'LL INCLUDE THEM IN THE FUN.
CHAIN THEM UP...

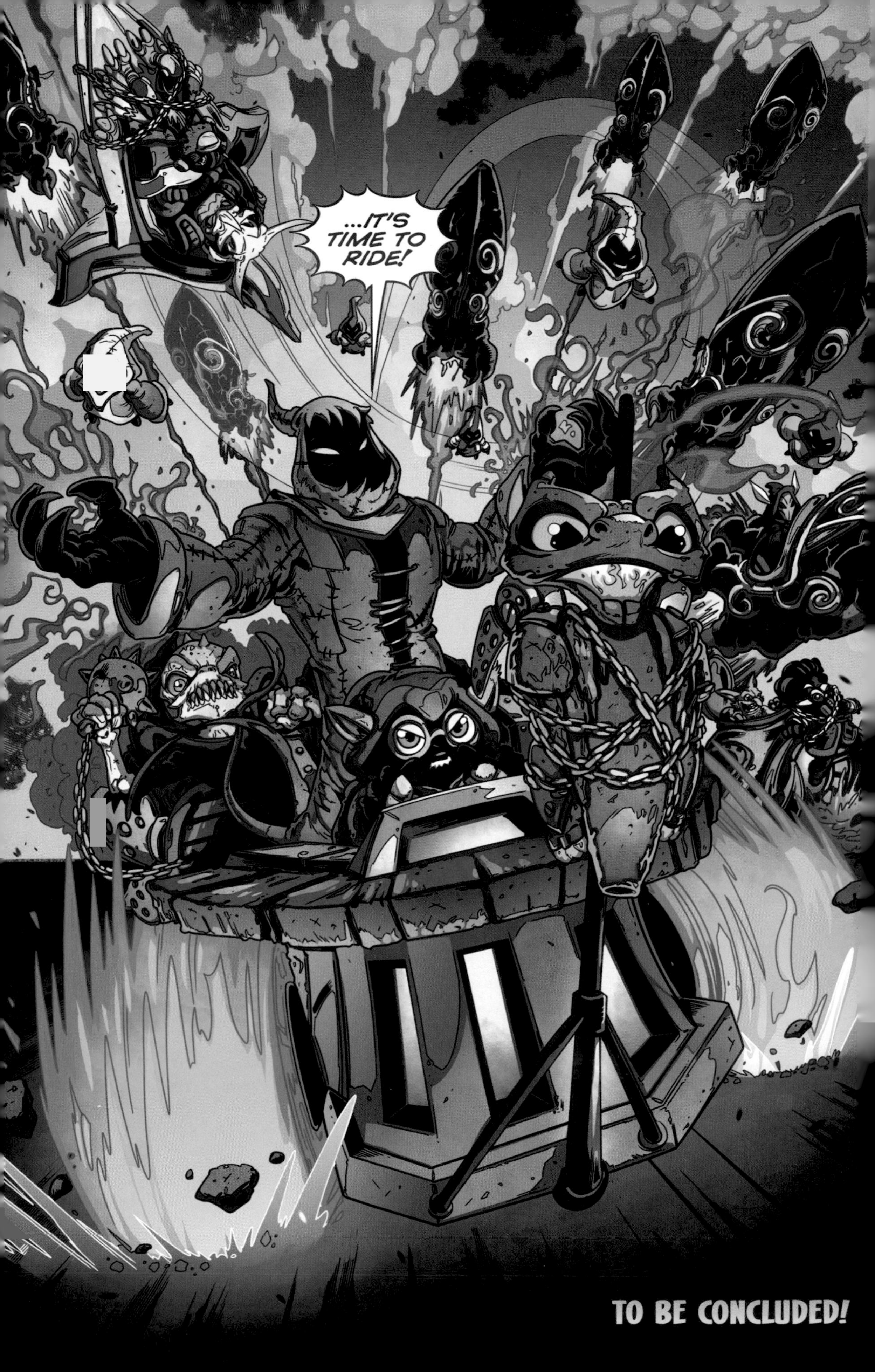
...IT'S TIME TO RIDE!
TO BE CONCLUDED!

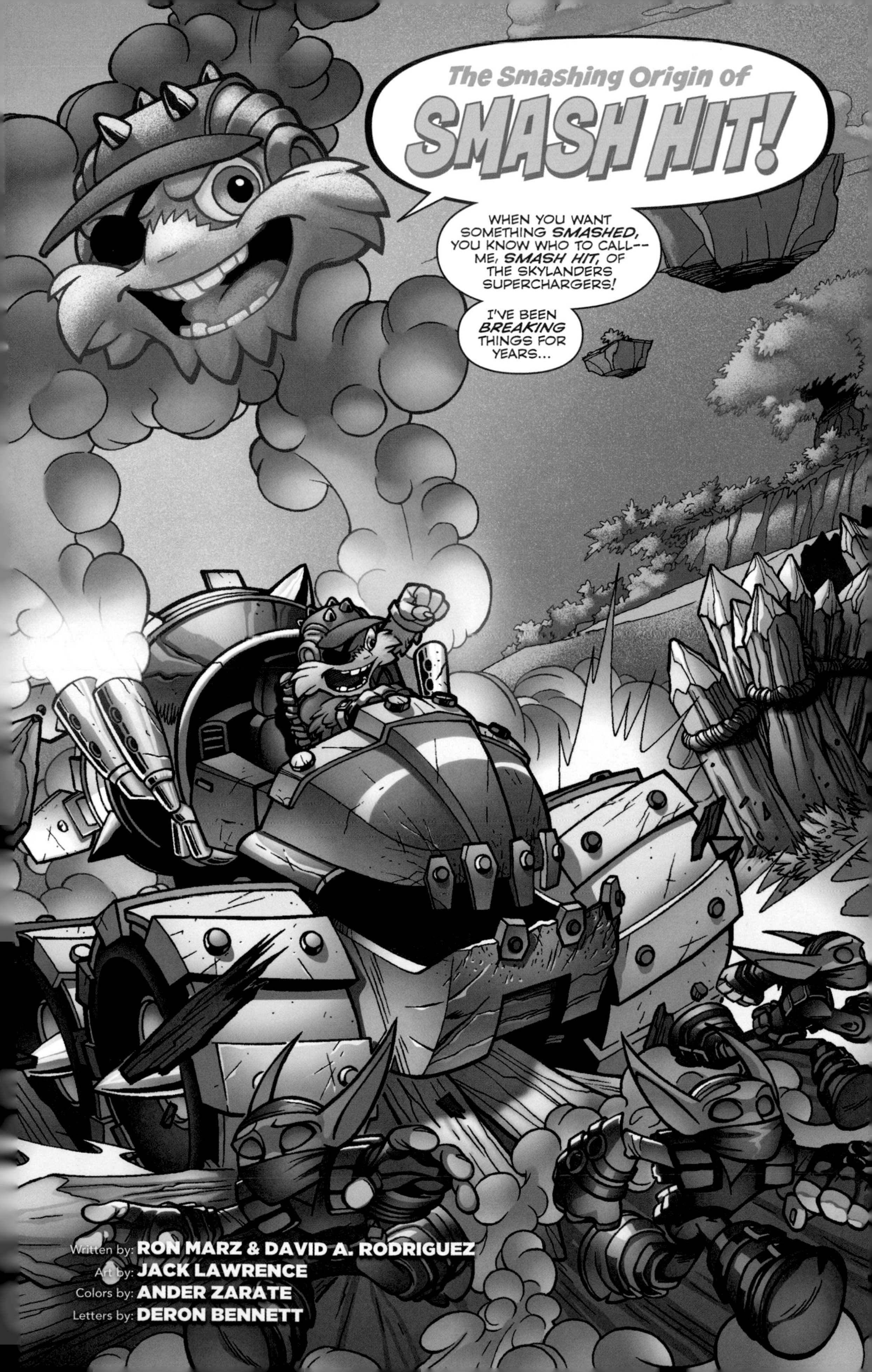
The Smashing Origin of
SMASH HIT!
WHEN YOU WANT SOMETHING SMASHED, YOU KNOW WHO TO CALL-- ME, SMASH HIT, OF THE SKYLANDERS SUPERCHARGERS!
I'VE BEEN BREAKING THINGS FOR YEARS...

Written by: **RON MARZ & DAVID A. RODRIGUEZ**
Art by: **JACK LAWRENCE**
Colors by: **ANDER ZARATE**
Letters by: **DERON BENNETT**

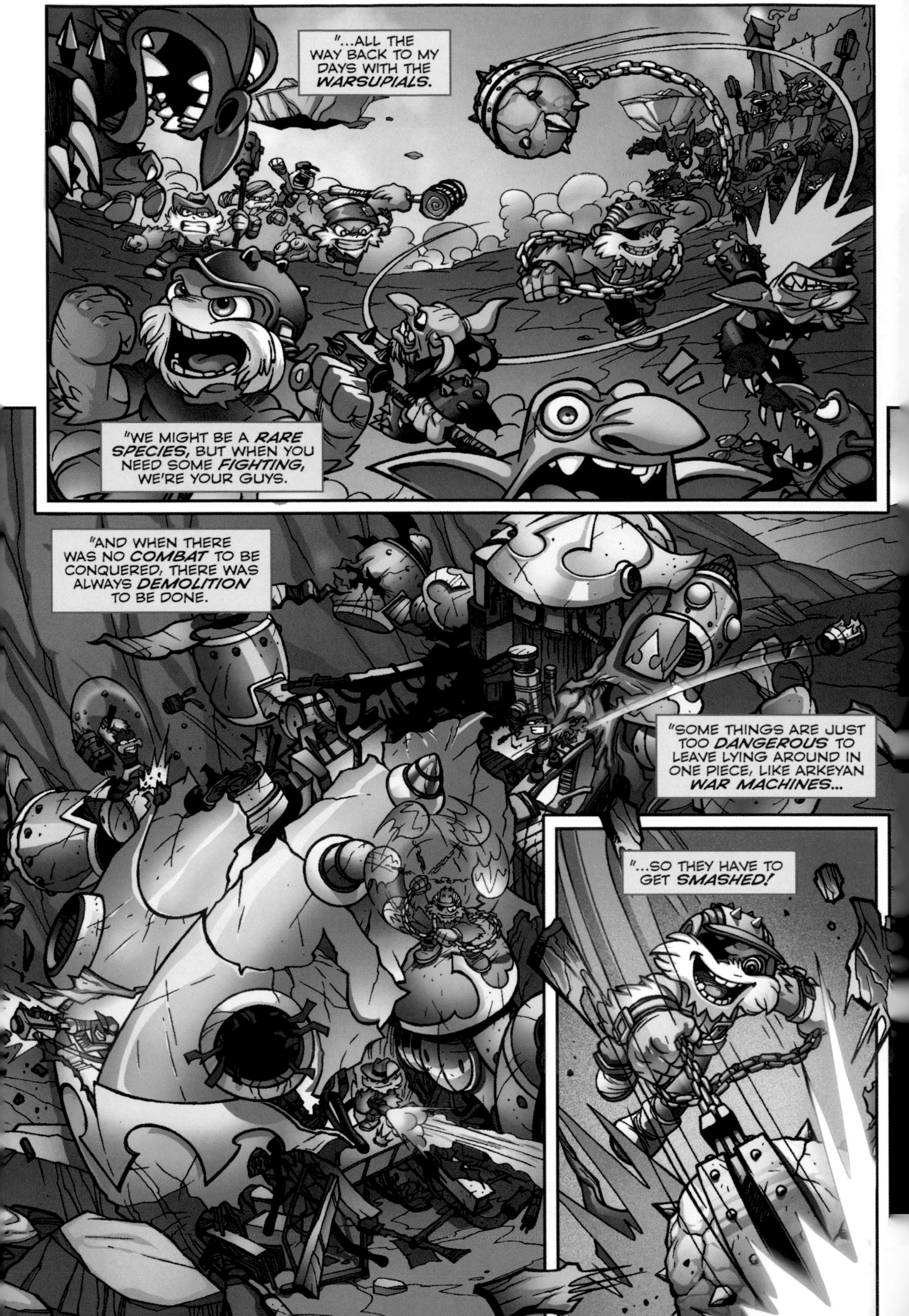
"...ALL THE WAY BACK TO MY DAYS WITH THE WARSUPIALS.
"WE MIGHT BE A RARE SPECIES, BUT WHEN YOU NEED SOME FIGHTING, WE'RE YOUR GUYS.
"AND WHEN THERE WAS NO COMBAT TO BE CONQUERED, THERE WAS ALWAYS DEMOLITION TO BE DONE.
"SOME THINGS ARE JUST TOO DANGEROUS TO LEAVE LYING AROUND IN ONE PIECE, LIKE ARKEYAN WAR MACHINES...
"...SO THEY HAVE TO GET SMASHED!

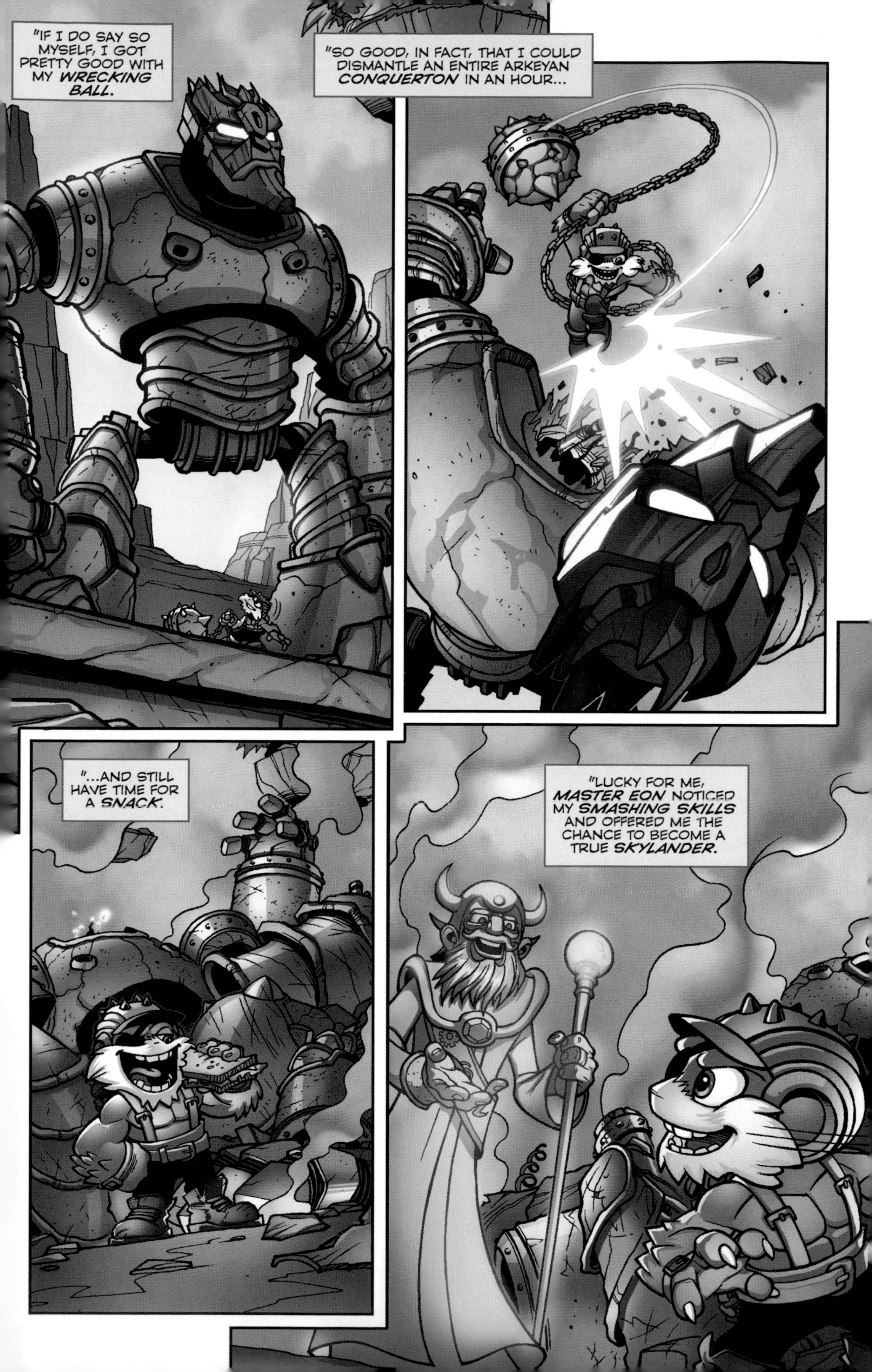
"IF I DO SAY SO MYSELF, I GOT PRETTY GOOD WITH MY WRECKING BALL.
"SO GOOD, IN FACT, THAT I COULD DISMANTLE AN ENTIRE ARKEYAN CONQUERTON IN AN HOUR...
"...AND STILL HAVE TIME FOR A SNACK.
"LUCKY FOR ME, MASTER EON NOTICED MY SMASHING SKILLS AND OFFERED ME THE CHANCE TO BECOME A TRUE SKYLANDER.

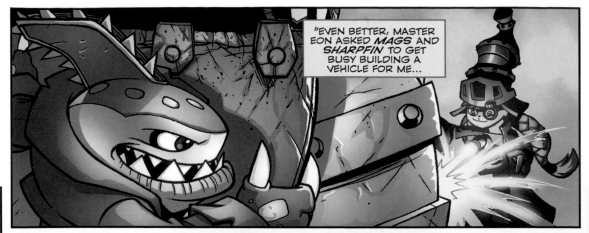

"EVEN BETTER, MASTER EON ASKED *MAGS* AND *SHARPFIN* TO GET BUSY BUILDING A VEHICLE FOR ME..."

"...AND THE RESULT WAS MY AMAZINGLY AWESOME *THUMP TRUCK!*"

"NOW I CAN ROLL OVER *ANY OBSTACLE* AND *EVERY OPPONENT...*"

"...ESPECIALLY WHEN I'M **SUPERCHARGED!**

HOW'S *THAT* FOR SMASHING?"

END

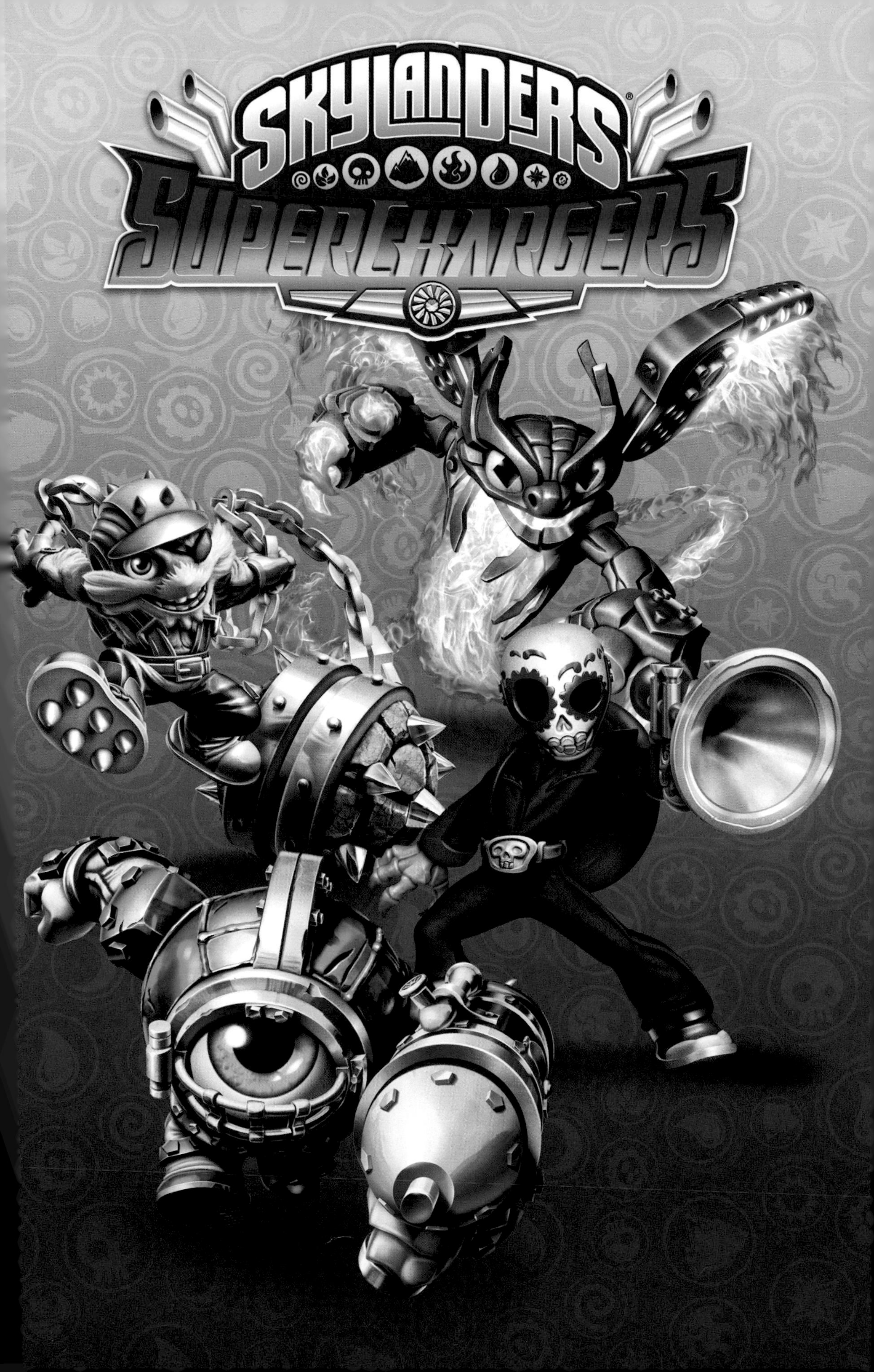
SKYLANDERS
SUPERCHARGERS

COLLECT THEM ALL!

Set of 6 Hardcover Books ISBN: 978-1-5321-4035-8

Hardcover Book ISBN
978-1-5321-4036-5

Hardcover Book ISBN
978-1-5321-4037-2

Hardcover Book ISBN
978-1-5321-4038-9

Hardcover Book ISBN
978-1-5321-4039-6

Hardcover Book ISBN
978-1-5321-4040-2

Hardcover Book ISBN
978-1-5321-4041-9